A SPY IN THE
NEIGHBORHOOD

A SPY IN THE NEIGHBORHOOD

Marjorie Weinman Sharmat

AN
APPLE
PAPERBACK

SCHOLASTIC INC.
New York Toronto London Auckland Sydney

ISBN 0-590-42633-8

Copyright © 1971 by Marjorie Weinman Sharmat. All rights reserved. Published by Scholastic Inc., 730 Broadway, New York, NY 10003, by arrangement with the author. APPLE PAPERBACKS is a registered trademark of Scholastic Inc.

12 11 10 9 8 7 6 5 4 3 2 1   9/8 0 1 2 3 4/9

Printed in the U.S.A.   40

First Scholastic printing, December 1989

Mostly for Craig and Andrew
(but a little bit for their chicken)

1

School starts tomorrow and I bet the first assignment in Miss Nathan's English class will be a composition titled "How I Spent My Summer Vacation." This would be my third year with the same title. If I were Miss Nathan I would try to come up with a different idea. As a boy gets older, how he spent his summer vacation gets to be more and more *his* business and less and less his teacher's. Take this summer, for example. I could probably write in one sentence about everything that happened before the week of July 12. But I think I would get writer's cramp trying to describe what went on during that week. Maybe I ended the week a little smarter than when I started it, which is the kind of thing English teachers like to read about. But that's the week Paul got me into the mess, and Miss Nathan is a tidy person who avoids messes of any sort.

Maybe Paul wasn't 100 percent to blame for getting me into the mess, but he was somewhere up there in the nineties. I'll explain about Paul. He is an "intellectually gifted child" and he has an IQ of about 150, give or take a little. All the mothers want their kids to play with him because they are hoping that whatever he's got is catching. And the kids *want* to play with him even though their mothers want them to. Paul is full of ideas and most of his ideas are fun.

Paul's parents are afraid that he will grow up to live in an ivory tower and be covered with dust and have a beard to the floor and no muscles and no friends. So they are very anxious for him to do "physical and menial" things, as they say. And that is why Paul plays football and takes lessons on the drums and has outside jobs.

And that's how he met Mrs. Richardson. And meeting Mrs. Richardson led to the mess.

A few weeks earlier Mrs. Richardson had moved to Sycamore Lane where Paul lives. Sycamore Lane is in a neighborhood where all the streets are named after trees and lakes to make sure the people realize they are living far away from the city. Paul rang Mrs. Richardson's bell and asked if she had any odd jobs. Mrs. Richardson looked him over and invited him in. She offered him a seat on a packing crate. Inside the crate was a large white chicken.

"I'm Mrs. Richardson," said Mrs. Richardson, "and this is Miss America."

"It's a pleasure to meet both of you," said Paul. He looked down into the crate. Miss America clucked.

"She loves company," said Mrs. Richardson.

"Am I sitting on her home?" asked Paul.

"Her temporary home," said Mrs. Richardson. "I've ordered her a splendid coop. Most of the time she's out of doors, though. That's the joy of a house. Children can romp outside."

"Children?" said Paul.

"Miss America is still a child," said Mrs. Richardson. "But she's growing fast. She'll be laying eggs before I know it. She was just a baby when I won her in a raffle. She was Prize Number 13, but I assure you she was the best prize. There she was, this dear little chicken, way down the list of prizes. After the color TV set, after the luggage, after the steam iron, after the matching set of pots and pans, after all kinds of *things*."

Suddenly Mrs. Richardson snapped to attention. So did Paul. She took out a notebook and started to write in it.

"Your name, please?"

"Paul H Botts. The *H* doesn't stand for anything as yet. My parents want me to select a middle name when I'm twenty-one. Right now it's a tie between Horatio and Horace."

"How much do you weigh, Paul?"

"Seventy-six pounds, two ounces," said Paul. "In the morning, unclothed."

"Height?" asked Mrs. Richardson.

"Fifty-six and one-half inches with my hair combed flat," said Paul.

"You'll do," said Mrs. Richardson. "Would you like a job walking my dog Melvin twice a day, once in the morning, once in the afternoon? The job starts next week, but you would need one training session. Tomorrow afternoon would be a good time, I think. The training session pays fifty cents and the job pays one dollar a day plus tips if you deserve them."

"Checks or currency?" asked Paul.

"Currency of course," said Mrs. Richardson. "What could you do with a check?"

"I would have it deposited to my account at the local savings bank, which pays interest at an annual rate of 5½ percent, posted quarterly and computed from the day of deposit," said Paul. "You might want to look into it."

"I don't trust banks," said Mrs. Richardson. "Most of my money is in the stock market and the rest is in a cookie jar and together they make a splendid combination. But you wouldn't know about things like that."

Actually Paul *did* know a lot about the stock market — and cookie jars — but he was eager to go ahead and ask his next question. "Why did you want to know my height and weight?"

"I have found that statistics prove invaluable," said Mrs. Richardson. "For example, Melvin weighs approximately 105 pounds. That is 29 pounds more than you, and he seems to be getting bigger by the hour. I keep him well fed. To protect the chicken, you know. However, considering your height and the fact that you were sufficiently enterprising to ask for a job, I have decided to hire you. Melvin might possibly knock you over a few times, but he means well. Does that answer your question?"

"Actually, it tells more than I really wanted to know," said Paul. "And you may be interested to learn that I also play football and the drums. My hair is light brown, which in the summer turns to the shade known as dirty blond. Around my forehead and eyes I am the spitting image of my Uncle Harry. I can wiggle my ears at will, but usually I refrain from doing so. All the teeth you see are my own."

"I already have the information I need," said Mrs. Richardson. "Now that we've settled everything, I'm having some coffee. Do you drink coffee?"

"My parents haven't made a decision on that yet," said Paul.

"Very well, I'll give you cocoa," said Mrs. Richardson.

Mrs. Richardson went into the kitchen to make the coffee and cocoa. Paul looked around. Mrs. Richardson was almost completely unpacked. Most of her furniture was somewhere between wearing out and worn out. The kind of furniture my mother calls "friendly." There was a wastebasket full of chicken feathers. There were notebooks everywhere. Paul guessed that she couldn't have had *that* many dog walkers before him. And there were piles of mail with foreign stamps and postmarks.

But it was the next thing that Paul saw that really got to him. In a corner almost hidden Paul saw *it*. It was a shortwave radio! Why would Mrs. Richardson have a shortwave radio? he asked himself. And then, because he liked ideas, Paul put the idea of the notebooks, the foreign mail and the shortwave radio together. At that moment Paul decided that Mrs. Richardson was a spy.

2

Mrs. Richardson came back to the room with coffee, cocoa and some cookies. "Here's your cocoa," she said. "Nice and hot. Don't burn yourself."

"Cocoa makes my face break out," said Paul. And he ran to the front door.

"That's a statistic I could have used before I made it," said Mrs. Richardson. "I'll see you tomorrow afternoon at 3 o'clock."

Paul ran all the way to my house. I live on Dartmouth Street, which is in an older part of town. It was there long before the woodsy and watery streets came along.

"I have absolutely chilling information," said Paul. "A spy has moved into 51 Sycamore Lane."

Then he told me the whole story. If anyone else had told me, I would have laughed it off. But, as I said, Paul is smart and he has a way of telling about things that makes them seem believable. And anyway, it had been a nothing summer so far, and this was *something*. It was a chance to be somebody besides myself. Like a detective. I had just seen a movie where a bunch of boys had solved a mystery in glowing color on a wide screen with everything looking gigantic and important and with nervous violins and beating drums and fantastic effects. After it was over and I was walking out, I got a glimpse of myself in the mirror of the theater lobby under the fluorescent lights. I looked like some kind of tiny, grayish-white, squinting, wishy-washy earth creature. Like a mouse with clothes on. I wanted to be like the boys on the screen even if nobody was going to supply all the trimmings. Paul was giving me my chance.

"You can count on me," I said. "What should we do first?"

"There is a certain amount of safety in numbers," said Paul. "So first we will call Quentin and tell him to come over. Then we will have three minds to work on this."

I knew even then that Paul's mind would be doing most of the work.

I called Quentin. I tried to make the conversation short. Quentin is not a telephone person. He lives on Dogwood Lane, which is next to Sycamore, but over the telephone he always has a weird, faraway sound in his voice as if he were in another world. As if maybe his body had died the day before yesterday, but his voice was still trying to carry on.

"Quentin," I said. "It's me. Come over right away. It's very important."

And the voice said, "Umm. All right."

In ten minutes he was at my house. Face to face Quentin is alive and O.K. He's about as different from Paul as anyone can get. Quentin uses his brains, too, but they are always going off in another direction from Paul's. Quentin is a guy who works very hard but doesn't always get results. For example, his face usually looks like it needs washing right after he washes it, and his hair usually looks like it needs combing right after he combs it. He sort of reminds me of a sheepdog who has been caught permanently in the middle of a meal of gravy. And he has one habit that Paul can't stand. Whenever he is very excited, Quentin says "Wow!"

But we're all pals, and we've been through plenty of trouble together. So it seemed right that we should go through this together now. Whatever this was.

Paul told the story all over again to Quentin and Quentin said "Wow!" Paul didn't seem to mind this time. It was really very easy to convince Quentin, for there were two of us doing the convincing.

We all went upstairs to my bedroom. And there,

with a bag of pretzels and some soda to help us think, we made our plans.

"First," said Paul, "we will try to get all the information we can about Mrs. Richardson without taking any risks. If that doesn't work, we will have to close in and keep her under constant surveillance until we have sufficient evidence to turn her over to the proper authorities. In this case, the FBI."

"You mean when we get the goods on her?" asked Quentin, who liked to translate Paul into our kind of English. I think I should mention that whenever Quentin and I look up Paul's big words in the dictionary, they are always there.

"Tomorrow afternoon Mrs. Richardson and I are taking her dog for a walk. By the time the walk is over, I hope to know quite a bit about Mrs. Richardson." Paul smiled. "Quite a bit." Then he said, "Now, while I am out with Mrs. Richardson I have an assignment for the two of you. Your assignment is Stella Verndale."

"Stella Verndale is an assignment?" asked Quentin. "Stella Verndale is a woman."

"Stella Verndale is a woman who lives next door to Mrs. Richardson," said Paul. "Stella Verndale is a woman who *talks*. *She* will talk about Mrs. Richardson. I guarantee it."

Paul looked straight at me. He was waiting for

me to catch on. I did. "Stella Verndale belongs to my mother's bridge club," I said. "And the club meets here tomorrow."

"That's right," said Paul. "Your mother is downstairs baking cookies for it. I know the bridge-club cookies aroma. You and Quentin can listen to Stella from the next room tomorrow."

"That won't be hard," I said. "You can hear Stella a block away."

"With earmuffs on," said Quentin.

"That completes the plans for tomorrow," said Paul. "I'm certain that I don't have to remind either of you to say absolutely nothing to anyone about this."

"If you're so certain, why did you remind us?" asked Quentin.

At suppertime I usually talk about things like baseball scores and baseball players. So in order not to make my parents suspicious, I talked about baseball scores and baseball players. But after a while I couldn't seem to help it and I mentioned Mrs. Richardson.

I tried to be very cool. I put some food in my mouth while I talked so as to split the attention between the subject of Mrs. Richardson and the subject of food in my mouth.

"What do you think of Mrs. Richardson?" I asked my mother.

"You've got food in your mouth," she said.

Then she said, "Mrs. Richardson is a nice person."

I don't know why I asked. My mother always says that about the kind of ladies who don't put a lot of stuff on their faces and don't throw noisy parties and always spread the word when there's a special at the butcher shop.

"How well do you know her?" I asked.

"Well, I really don't know her. I know *of* her," said my mother.

"Your mother's bridge club knows of her," said my father. "And that's good enough for your mother."

My father always kidded my mother about her bridge club, and my mother always pretended to mind. I didn't think it was so funny. The ladies in the club were like a mixture of pizza and whipped cream and French fries and taffy. Separately they were fine, but when they got together they were awful. Except for Stella Verndale who was awful all by herself.

My mother opened her mouth to say something but my father opened his quicker. "Why do you want to know about Mrs. Richardson?" he asked. "Did you break her window or something?"

"No," I said. "In fact I'm really not interested in her at all. I was just making conversation. I get tired of talking about baseball sometimes."

I put a huge load of food in my mouth.

But my father didn't notice. "Did you break her window?" he asked again.

"No," I said. "I just think that when people move to town, the people who were there first should pay attention to them. Like the Welcome Wagon, but without the business side of it."

I knew I was talking too much but I didn't know how to stop. Paul would have known how to get out of this conversation. Paul wouldn't have gotten *into* it.

"I got a B plus on my last history test," I said, giving myself a D minus on the conversation. I could see that my father was still thinking about broken windows.

"That's wonderful," said my mother. "And I thought it was wonderful in June when you first told us about it." Then she said to my father, "Now what was that about my bridge club, Max?"

And that was the end of Mrs. Richardson at the supper table for that night.

When I went to bed I fell asleep fast. I was very surprised the next morning to remember that I didn't have a spy dream. The dream I remembered was all about broken windows.

3

I hung around the house until Quentin came over after lunch. Then we went to the den, which is next to the living room, which is where the bridge club was going to meet. We pretended to read magazines, and my mother didn't pay any attention to us because we were quiet.

The club meets once a month at the home of a member. There are about twelve members, but usually a few don't show up. If I belonged to the same club as Stella Verndale I would *never* show up. But today Quentin and I were practically praying she would come.

And she did. She was the last person to arrive. I think she was always the last person to arrive. Like she was the star of a show and she wanted to make sure the audience was settled in first.

Stella said hello to everyone and sat down at a table.

My mother said, "How have you been, Stella?"

"I could be better," said Stella. "Much better."

"I'm sorry to hear that," said my mother. "Well, let's start playing."

The ladies picked up their cards. All except Stella. She was all ready with an answer to a question nobody was asking. The trouble with asking Stella questions was that the answers might take most of the afternoon. One afternoon I heard her spend two hours complaining about her headache and the humidity. What Stella needed in her life was someone who would signal when three minutes were up and who would charge her overtime if she kept on talking.

Stella looked around the table. She said, "I could be a lot better, I'll tell you that."

"What's wrong?" asked one of the ladies finally.

"Don't ask," said Stella.

"All right," said the lady.

"I'll tell you," said Stella. "Do you know that I now live next door to a chicken?"

Quentin and I put our ears on full alert. Stella was talking about Mrs. Richardson's chicken. We were in luck. It could have been another headache and humidity day.

Stella went on. "That Mrs. Richardson who moved in next door to me — that strange, strange woman. She's got a dog that's not an inch under the size of King Kong, but at least he's on a leash. This chicken she's got — this *hen* she calls Miss America — runs loose all over my property cluck-

clucking like a — like a — *hen*. I chase her away, but she comes back. She ate the leaves off one of my plants and the berries off another. And what she's done to my lawn — don't ask. She's dropped so many feathers on it you'd think my grass had been in a pillow fight. And dirty, you wouldn't believe how dirty she is."

Stella clutched her head with one hand and took a piece of candy with the other. I felt grateful to her for her big mouth. Paul had said she would talk about Mrs. Richardson, and that's what she was doing. Stella was certainly a person you could depend upon if you knew what part of her to depend upon.

"Have you spoken to Mrs. Richardson about her chicken?" asked my mother.

"Let me tell you I did," said Stella. "I marched myself right up to her house and told her that I didn't want any dirty chicken on my property. And do you know what she said to me? Get this for nerve. She said that I was insulting Miss America. How can you insult a chicken, I ask you. Anyway, I've got a better way to handle this. Listen, when I wage war why should I use just one soldier when I can get a whole regiment?"

"What do you mean?" asked my mother.

"I mean *this*," said Stella. She took a piece of paper from her pocketbook and kept unfolding it.

It was very long. "I've written a petition to get rid of the chicken," she said. "And I'm hoping that the whole neighborhood will sign it. And of course I want you girls to be first. I tell you I never knew I had the talent in me to write such a thing. If only they gave a Pulitzer Prize for petitions."

My mother said, "Let's play first and discuss the petition later. I'll put it in the dining room with the food so we won't forget it."

Stella looked disappointed. But she picked up her cards and started to play.

Quentin and I smiled at each other, shook our heads up and down in agreement, tiptoed into the dining room and snatched the petition off the buffet where my mother had put it. Some of the ladies in the living room saw us do it, but nobody said a word. They were on the chicken's side. Quentin and I took the petition to the den and read it fast.

"ALL THAT IS NECESSARY FOR THE FORCES OF EVIL TO WIN IN THE WORLD IS FOR ENOUGH GOOD MEN TO DO NOTHING."
                    — Edmund Burke

We, the undersigned, wish to protest the presence of the chicken known as Miss America who resides with Mrs. Ethel

17

Richardson at 51 Sycamore Lane. She is a health hazard and a public nuisance, constantly producing unsanitary conditions, consuming plants and flowers, erupting feathers and clucking incessantly. We strongly urge her immediate removal.

Stella Verndale

"She wants to do in Miss America," said Quentin. "Wow!"

We put the petition back on the buffet. I wanted to tear it up but I didn't dare. Once and for all and forever I hated Stella Verndale. Maybe way down inside her there was something kind and good, but it was hidden so deep you'd have to hire an excavation team to go down and find it and bring it up to the daylight.

Quentin said, "Wait till we tell Paul." And then he said, "Wait till we tell Paul *what*? We haven't found out anything about Mrs. Richardson that we didn't already know."

Quentin was right. And we didn't do any better for the rest of the bridge game. The ladies read the petition and told Stella that they couldn't sign anything without discussing it first with their husbands. They were probably hoping that she would calm down by the next meeting and forget the chicken.

Paul came along just as the ladies were leaving. He had less to report than we did. Mrs. Richardson had talked only about her dog. "Two hours of straight dog-talk," said Paul. "She paid me overtime. And she gave me a tip each time the dog knocked me over."

"At least you got paid," said Quentin. "All we got was chicken-talk from Stella Bigmouth."

And he told Paul all about Stella and the petition.

Paul got excited. "This is very significant information," he said.

"It is?" asked Quentin.

"Very significant," said Paul. "If Stella takes this petition around the neighborhood, people are going to be curious about Mrs. Richardson. They'll pass her house and point to it and say, 'The chicken lady lives here.' And some of them might hang around to get a look at her. She'll probably get mentioned in the local newspaper. In a town like this, almost anything is news."

Paul was right. When I fell down and broke my left wrist, I got mentioned on page 4 of the paper. My name and street were spelled wrong and my age was printed upside down, but I got twelve telephone calls, fifteen get-well cards and a free half-gallon of ice cream from the pharmacy. I suppose if I had broken both wrists I would have done even better.

"That's not all," said Paul. "There's always the danger that pro-chicken and anti-chicken groups will form and start descending on Mrs. Richardson's house."

Paul knew all about pro and anti groups. At one time or another his mother has been chairman of the Pro-Cleaner Water, Pro-Dump the Mayor and Pro-New Benches for the Railroad Station committees as well as chairman of the Anti-Air Pollution, Anti-Horn Honking and Anti-New Furnishings for Town Hall committees.

"If that petition starts circulating," said Paul, "it will stir things up. How can we investigate Mrs. Richardson with people there all the time? We've got to stop that petition!"

Paul was showing real pioneer spirit. He had staked out Mrs. Richardson's territory for the three of us and he wasn't going to let the town overrun it.

"How are we going to stop the petition?" asked Quentin.

"By paying a visit to Stella Verndale," said Paul.

"By *you* paying a visit to Stella Verndale," said Quentin. "I'm going home."

"If you don't come with us, every time you eat a chicken dinner you will wonder who are you eating," said Paul, "and you will never be sure."

"I don't even know Miss America," said Quentin.

"But you know Stella Verndale," said Paul. "Do you want her to win?"

"I'm coming," said Quentin.

4

We waited until Stella had time to get home. Then we walked to her house. Paul rang her bell. Quentin and I kept staring at the house next door. 51 Sycamore Lane. The Spy House. It had tan shingles and brick and rhododendron. For a spy house, it certainly wasn't anything special.

Stella opened her door and said, "I just bought some from the last kids who were around."

"Bought what?" I asked.

"Whatever you're selling," said Stella. She started to close the door.

"We're not selling anything," said Paul. "We came about your petition."

Stella stopped closing the door. "What about my petition?" she asked.

"We'd like to come in and discuss it," said Paul. "We have a very valuable suggestion to make." He stuck his foot in the opening made by the almost-closed door. I once saw a salesman do that

22

to my mother and she landed up with a new vacuum cleaner she didn't need.

"Tell me here on the porch," said Stella. "It will be just as valuable."

"Inside," said Paul.

"All right, come in," said Stella. "But it better be good."

Stella led us through the living room into what could be called either a tiny room or a huge closet. Paul, Quentin and I sat down on a small sofa.

"Well?" said Stella. She looked mad and Paul hadn't even said anything yet. The visit was having what is known as a shaky beginning.

Paul said, "Do you know that a chicken is truly a gentle bird, a noble bird, a bird with a background rich in history, a bird with — "

Stella interrupted. "This is a valuable suggestion?"

"I will continue," said Paul. "Going back in history, we have such eminent chicken owners as Cleopatra — "

"Cleopatra?" said Stella.

"Yes, indeed," said Paul. His eyes seemed to be fixed on something straight across the room. Stella's bookshelves. She had two rows of books about famous people, in alphabetical order. Paul went on. "Also Disraeli, Ivan the Terrible, Thomas Jefferson, Genghis Khan, Abraham Lincoln, King Louis XII, XIII and XIV, Marilyn Monroe, Nero, Marco Polo, Betsy Ross, Shakespeare, Rudolph Valentino and George Washington. They all owned chickens."

"Really?" said Stella. She seemed a little impressed. I guess she didn't pay much attention to her books, inside or out. I wondered if some winter night when it was very cold and she had nothing else to do she might glance over her books and then remember Paul's list of chicken owners. Boy, I'd like to see her face.

Paul said, "You really do not want to persecute a fine, historical bird like that, do you?"

Now Stella was really mad. "Cleopatra's chickens didn't bother me, or Thomas Jefferson's or the King of Siam's," she practically yelled.

"I don't think the King of Siam had any chickens," said Quentin.

Stella was fuming. "It's that Mrs. Richardson's chicken," she said. "That cluck-cluck of a pest."

Now Quentin got mad. "*You* cluck-cluck, too," he said, "and nobody is getting up a petition against *you!*"

I won't say that Stella exactly swept us out the front door, but she sort of swooped down and gathered us up and moved us in that direction. At the same time she said "Scram!"

Actually that was quite a valuable suggestion. We left.

"I'm not sorry, I'm not sorry," said Quentin as we walked down Sycamore Lane. "You know who the real hen is? It's Stella. She *does* cluck-cluck."

I was a little jealous of Quentin. He had come right out and spoken the truth straight to Stella's face. Quentin was really brave. I wasn't sure that I was. I wanted to go back and ring Stella's bell and when she opened the door I would say, "*I* think you cluck-cluck, too."

"I'm going back and tell her off," I said.

"No, you're not," said Paul. "Quentin took care of that nicely. You *did*, Quentin. However, the truth can be costly, and that cluck-cluck conversation spoiled our chance to reason with Stella. Not that we had much of a chance. We need someone really important to go after her. Someone she'll look up to and *fear*."

"How about the President of the United States?" asked Quentin.

Paul didn't answer him.

"Of General Motors or General Electric?" asked Quentin.

Those were the only other American presidents he had heard of lately.

"We need a lawyer," said Paul. "From the city. From New York City. *That* will shake up Stella."

"How are we going to get someone like that?" I asked.

"The way anybody else does," said Paul. "We simply make a telephone call."

"Sure," said Quentin. "That's the way it's done. Even criminals get to make one phone call when they're arrested and they always call their lawyer. If I were arrested, I would call my mother and let her call the lawyer. That way I would get two phone calls for one."

"We'll go to my house," said Paul, "and telephone from there. It won't cost us anything."

Paul's parents had a twenty-five-mile rule for his telephone calls. Under twenty-five miles, they paid. Over twenty-five miles came out of his allowance, unless he was calling relatives. Paul said they made the rule just to prevent him from calling a good friend of his in Memphis, Tennessee.

Paul's mother wasn't home when we got to his house. Paul went straight to the Manhattan telephone directory, which was underneath several other telephone books. He opened it and turned some pages until he got to the *F*'s. "Here we are," he said. "Fuller, Fox, Alpert, Hirsch, Hollingsworth & Emple. On Madison Avenue." He wrote down a number and started to dial.

"How do you know what lawyer to call?" I asked.

"I *read*," he said. "I *read*. Do you know which baseball teams are in the big leagues?"

"Sure," I said.

"Well, I know which law firms are." Then he spoke into the receiver. "This is Mr. Paul H Botts speaking. I am in urgent need of legal assistance."

Paul's voice was suddenly about one octave lower and ten years older than usual. He sounded at least old enough to vote. I was surprised. He used to say that disguises of any type were childish. In fact, Halloween was his idea of a dirty word.

"Who referred me? Madam, any aware person has heard of Fuller, Fox, Alpert, Hirsch, Hollingsworth & Emple. When can I have an appointment?"

There was a long wait. Paul cleared his throat down in his new octave. Then he said. "Three weeks? Madam, perhaps you didn't hear me before. This is an emergency. I'm willing to be squeezed in between other appointments if necessary."

There was another long wait. Then Paul said, "Eleven-ten tomorrow with Mr. Emple. Very good. Yes, Botts. Two *t*'s. Mr. Paul H Botts. *H* as in Horatio or Horace. Thank you, madam. Good-bye."

Paul hung up and turned to us. "We're all set," he said in his natural voice. But Quentin and I were laughing too hard to answer. "Wow, was that a conversation?" said Quentin. "And, boy, is that madam dumb? I'd sure love to see what she's like in person."

"You will," said Paul. "The three of us are going into the city tomorrow."

"That's what you think," I said. "We haven't even asked our mothers if we can go."

"No problem," said Paul. "I'll take care of my mother and she'll take care of your mothers. We'll take the 9:36 train to New York. If the train runs on schedule we will arrive in New York at 10:25. It should take about fifteen minutes to walk to the law office. So we will probably get there at 10:40, which will be thirty minutes early. However, if the train is late, we might need that thirty minutes."

"You're sure that we're going, aren't you?" I said.

"Absolutely," said Paul. "Absolutely. Tell your mothers to expect a call from my mother tonight."

"You're not going to tell your mother about the spy angle, are you?" I asked.

"Never," said Paul. "I'll concentrate on the chicken and justice. My mother is pleased that there's a chicken on the street. She always wanted me to have a rural experience."

"Wait a minute," said Quentin. "Let's talk about the spy angle. Let's talk about the spy. I don't want to see a lawyer. I want to go after the spy."

"We *are* going after her," said Paul.

"In New York City when she lives *here*?" asked Quentin.

"As soon as we take care of this petition problem, we can turn our attention completely to Mrs. Richardson," said Paul. "However, if you wish, we can take a vote on this matter. The majority vote wins. We can go to New York tomorrow or we can stay here and start working on a case we will probably never to able to finish if we don't go to New York first."

"I vote to stay here and start working on a case we will probably never be able to finish if we don't go to New York first," said Quentin. "At least we can start it."

"That's your privilege," said Paul. "You realize, of course, that a vote for the New York trip is a vote against Stella Verndale."

Quentin said, "I vote to change my vote."

Paul never got around to asking for my vote. He didn't need it.

I went home. My father was working late that night, so there was just my mother and I at supper. I told her what had happened at Stella's house. I started to tell her about the trip, but I didn't want to say too much until Paul's mother called. And she did. Right between the stew and the Jell-O.

I listened to my mother's end of the conversation. She seemed to be repeating what Mrs. Botts was saying. "Worthwhile," "broadening," "a legal experience," "justice," "see democrary at work." Then my mother said "uh-huh," "right," "I agree," "true." The conversation took about three or four minutes and when it was over my mother said to me, "If your father agrees, you can go."

Paul's mother was an even faster persuader than Paul.

My mother called my father at work and repeated her conversation with Mrs. Botts. I think the part about democracy at work made a big impression on my father, and when my mother threw in the word "justice" she had it made.

She said to me, "You can go."

I called Paul and told him I could definitely go. I wasn't a bit surprised when he told me that Quentin's mother had said yes, too.

My mother gave me instructions that Mrs. Botts had worked out. We were not to speak to anybody on the street unless we were lost. If we got lost, we were to ask a policeman for directions. If there wasn't a policeman around, we could ask any lady. But we couldn't ask a man unless he was wearing a suit, had neat hair, a shaved face and was carrying a briefcase. We had to take the next train back after the appointment. It would probably be the 12:20.

My mother helped me lay out my clothes for

the next day. And she polished my shoes. She acted as if I were going to Europe. I had been in New York City quite a few times but always with her and my father. She had seemed real pepped up about my trip when she talked to Mrs. Botts and my father, but it was starting to wear off. I was afraid it would be all worn off by morning and she would tell me I couldn't go. "Don't worry," I said. "I'll be with Quentin and *Paul*." I said "Paul" loud and clear. My mother cheered up. Sometimes she thought Paul was about sixty years old, and that was certainly old enough to take two kids to the city.

I went to bed early. If you go to bed early and fall asleep right away, morning seems to come sooner. The ring of the telephone woke me at seven the next morning. It was Paul. He was all wound up. "We have a perfect day," he said. "The radio reports that the skies are clear and sunny in mid-Manhattan and that the trains are running only five minutes behind schedule. My mother is driving Quentin and me to the station. Do you want her to pick you up, too?"

"No," I said. "But thanks anyway. I like the walk."

I live nearer to the station than Paul and Quentin. The walk is downhill all the way and it goes through an old tunnel and past a park that has a pond with two ducks in it. When I'm the only person in the tunnel, I can hear the echo of my feet and I feel all alone in the world. I thought it would be fun to take that kind of walk and then in the same day to walk in a busy place like New York City.

My father was still sleeping so I had breakfast with my mother. She was back to acting as if my trip was the kind I should send her a postcard from. "Perhaps you could take a later train and go in with your father when he goes to work," she said.

"*Paul* already has an appointment at 11:10," I said. "*Paul* can't break it now."

My mother repeated the instructions all over again. This time she said that the man we could ask directions from had to be wearing glasses, too.

I left my house at nine o'clock. My father was just getting up. He shook hands with me, and my mother kissed me twice. I was sure they would be talking about this day for years to come. They would start off saying, "Remember when . . ." They hadn't had a day like this since I went off to kindergarten.

I enjoyed the walk to the station, but it seemed odd to look down and see shiny black shoes instead of sneakers kicking the pebbles near the pond. I told the ducks where I was going. I always tell them something when I go by, if I'm alone. When I got to the station, Mrs. Botts was dropping off

Paul and Quentin. She gave Paul only one kiss.

Paul, Quentin and I sat on one of the benches near the track and waited for the train. The bench was broken in a few places and felt uncomfortable. I wondered if I was too young to join Mrs. Botts's Pro-New Benches for the Railroad Station committee. A train came along but it whizzed by on an inner track. Nine thirty-six came and went. So did nine thirty-seven, eight and nine. At nine forty-five we were still sitting on the bench.

"The train is already nine minutes late," I said.

"I know, I know," said Paul and he muttered something about inaccuracy in radio communications. Then he went on to inefficiency in running trains on schedule.

"Why don't you curse?" asked Quentin.

Some of the people waiting around had taken up Quentin's suggestion even before he made it. Suddenly we saw and heard a train coming around the bend toward us. It stopped in front of us. It was our train.

"Nine fifty-two," said Paul. "Sixteen minutes late. We now have just fourteen minutes to spare. If this train doesn't make good time, we're in trouble."

I thought it was exciting to have just fourteen minutes to spare instead of thirty minutes to kill. We got on a car that had a No Smoking sign. We sat three together. We let Quentin sit next to the window. He got there first anyway.

The train started up. I've always loved the feeling of sitting and having a machine move me forward. Like a car or bus. I liked the train the best because I didn't have a chance to ride on it very often. The conductor came along and we bought round-trip tickets. He put little tickets in the slots in front of our seats and gave each of us a larger size ticket for the trip back.

"Can I keep both tickets?" asked Quentin.

"No," said Paul. "The conductor collects both of them. One near the end of this trip. One on the trip back."

Quentin liked to collect souvenirs wherever he went. He especially liked printed pieces of paper. When he went shopping, the first thing he did was to pull out from pockets of clothes the tiny slips of paper that say inspected by a person or a number. He had two "Inspected by Anna," one by Kate, one by Frances, one by Minnie and one by Sam. He also had "Inspected by No. 3" and 10, 55, 80 and 96. Sometimes he would take the slips out of clothes he wasn't even buying and go ask the salesclerk if he could keep them, and the salesclerk usually shrugged and said, "Sure, kid."

Paul looked at his watch. "I think we're going to make it on time," he said.

"I don't understand this trip," said Quentin.

"You voted for it," said Paul.

"I voted against Stella," said Quentin. "I bet that right now Mrs. Richardson is spying her head off back home."

I didn't feel like talking. Mrs. Richardson and her spying and the chicken and the petition seemed far away. The trip was here. The trip was now. The trip was everything. We were moving past buildings and trees and along the Hudson River. I counted the boats I saw on the river. I guess I would have liked a boat ride even better than the train. Most of the other people in the car weren't paying any attention to the ride. They were reading or talking to each other as if they weren't moving along. I suppose I would have been that way, too, if I rode the train a lot. At every stop more people got on and crowded down the aisles and the train started to fill up. After the stop at Yonkers there weren't many seats left.

Quentin wanted to talk. "What do we do after we get to the lawyer's?" he asked. "After we shake hands and say how do you do and nice place you have here, if it *is* nice. Then what?"

"We will tell him about the petition and request him to write a letter to Stella Verndale to stop it. It's a very simple matter," said Paul.

"Are you going to tell him about Mrs. Richardson being a spy?" asked Quentin.

"Of course not," said Paul. "I'm not even going to mention her name unless absolutely necessary.

The petition is directed against Miss America."

"Won't this law stuff cost a lot of money?" asked Quentin.

"I imagine that there will be a legal fee," said Paul. "Don't worry about it."

"What do you mean, don't worry?" said Quentin. "Who's going to pay it?"

"We are, of course," said Paul. "We all get allowances. We can pay a little each week."

"For the next 989 weeks," said Quentin. "What happens if we don't pay? When you eat in a restaurant, if you don't have the money I think they make you wash dishes. What does a lawyer make you do?"

Paul didn't answer.

"I suppose I could vacuum his rugs and dust his furniture and law books," said Quentin.

"Look, there is New York ahead of us," said Paul.

Look, there is New York ahead of us, was Paul's way of telling Quentin to stop asking questions. We all kept quiet after that. It was quite a while before the tall buildings that had been ahead of us were beside us. Then the train went down into a very dark tunnel and we knew we would soon be pulling into Grand Central Station. Paul jumped up, ready to leave the train the moment it stopped. He looked at his watch. "It will be close," he said. "Close."

5

The train stopped and we ran out. We were rude, I think, pushing ahead of people. My mother says that's what the city does to people — makes them rude — but we had just arrived. Paul rushed ahead of us, and we followed as fast as we could. We went up a ramp and then up some stairs until we were in the gigantic main room. I was still following close behind Paul, but Quentin veered off to the left. He had seen rows and rows of timetables at an information booth and was grabbing some with both hands. Paul marched over and yanked him away. Quentin stuffed the timetables into his pockets. We followed Paul — straight ahead, right, left, and up a ramp — until at last we all joined the outside world. Paul turned to the right. "Hurry," he said. We crossed one street and kept walking until we reached a very busy intersection and had to wait for the Walk sign. I had time to look up at the street sign. We were at 42nd Street and Madison Avenue.

"I wonder what it's like to live in the city," I said.

"I used to live here," said Paul. "On East 57th Street. Up that way. A few blocks from Bloomingdale's. My father said that my mother actually lived at Bloomingdale's and that it would have to go out of business if we moved. But we moved and it didn't.

"The fantastic thing about the city," said Paul, "is that wherever you decide to go in it, there are always so very many other people who have decided to go to the same place at the same time."

As we stood on the corner, I knew what Paul meant. There were loads of people heading for our corner, and there were plenty of people already there. I felt lucky to have a place to stand. It was like a game of musical chairs. Step quickly and try to find a place for yourself.

The Walk sign went on. We crossed Madison Avenue and started uptown. Quentin and I had to walk fast to keep up with Paul. We crossed more streets and waited on more corners.

"Why did you move?" I asked Paul.

"Bloomingdale's ran out of merchandise," said Quentin. And he laughed.

"My mother always wanted a house in the suburbs," said Paul, walking still faster. "For years she read ads on the real estate pages of *The New York Times*. My father said that everybody should have a hobby and if reading real estate ads was hers, it was fine with him. I think he also liked it because it was less expensive than yoga lessons and oil painting classes. One day it stopped being a hobby. My mother was intrigued by an ad for a particular house, she took a train to the suburbs, saw the house, wanted it, paid a deposit on it and told my father when he got home from work."

"What did your father do?" I asked.

Quentin piped up. "Have you ever seen a grown man faint?"

Suddenly Paul said, "We're here! This is the building."

"Finish your story," I said. "What happened between your mother and father?"

"To summarize," said Paul as we walked into the lobby of the building, "we're now living on Sycamore Lane in suburbia."

"What's your mother's hobby now?" asked Quentin.

Paul walked up to a huge directory on the wall of the lobby. "Fuller, Fox, Alpert, Hirsch, Hollingsworth & Emple," he read. "They're on the tenth floor."

We got into an elevator that had a sign saying I-II. There were a few people in it already and more got in. Paul, Quentin and I squashed together. Paul pressed the 10 button. The elevator started to move up. I sized up the other people. I always do that when I'm in an elevator. I try to figure out whether they would be good people to get stuck with. Mostly this group looked pretty good. There was one smiling man who would probably tell jokes until help came. But there was a fidgety lady who I knew would scream the whole time we were stuck. Paul was watching the numbers of the floors light up as we reached each one. When 10 lit up, he grabbed Quentin who would have gone on to 11 I'm sure.

"This way," said Paul. There was a double door to the right marked FULLER, FOX, ALPERT, HIRSCH, HOLLINGSWORTH & EMPLE in gold letters. Paul looked at his watch. "Exactly 11:10," he said. "Phenomenal."

Paul opened the door and we walked into a huge room colored green and gray. Quentin immediately said "Wow!"

The room was fixed up like it was back in the seventeenth or nineteenth century. It had a thick green rug, fancy dark furniture and paintings of a wrinkly sea captain, a vase of flowers, a snowy village and an overweight king and queen.

There was a lady sitting at a desk and switchboard. She was wearing glasses and her hair was pulled back tight like the ladies in some of the stories in my mother's magazines. In the stories, when the lady takes off her glasses and unpins her hair she becomes beautiful instantly. I didn't think that idea would work on this lady. She was dressed in a green and gray dress that seemed to come from the same place as everything else in the room. Whoever had picked out the furnishings must have picked her out at the same time.

We walked toward her desk. The room was so big I got the feeling that she was marooned on an island and we were crossing a green sea to rescue her. She was using the switchboard. She was telling someone named Rose that she would meet her at Schrafft's for lunch. She looked up and saw us. "Yes?" she said. Her words were aimed at us but her mind was having lunch at Schrafft's with Rose.

"I am Paul H Botts," said Paul, "and I have an 11:10 appointment with Mr. Emple."

"You do?" said the lady. "There must be some mistake."

"A mistake?" I said. All of a sudden I felt like what the grown-ups call a second-class citizen. Paul had told her his true name and the true facts of his appointment, and all she could say was, "There must be some mistake." I haven't been to many offices, but when I'm at the doctor's with my mother and my mother gives her name and appointment time at the front desk, she is usually told to please have a seat or please go right into the doctor's office. She is never told, "There must be some mistake."

41

"I am Paul H Botts and I have an 11:10 appointment with Mr. Emple," said Paul again. "And if you want to get back to Rose before she hangs up on you, I suggest that you buzz Mr. Emple and tell him I'm here."

Paul was beautiful. That's what he was. Beautiful.

The lady buzzed Mr. Emple. She said to Paul, "He'll be with you in a few minutes." I wondered, was she or wasn't she going to stick her tongue out at him next? She wasn't. She went back to Rose, but Rose had hung up.

Quentin whispered to Paul, "Is that madam?"

"Shh," said Paul.

Quentin was looking down at a high, neat pile of printed papers on the desk. "Are you giving these away, madam?" he asked. "Can I take one free?"

Paul pulled Quentin away before Madam Green-and-Gray could answer. The three of us sat down on a curvy bench. There were a couple of men also waiting in the room. They looked very rich, very old and very clean.

"Hey, here are some men we can ask directions from," said Quentin. "Except we're not lost."

We picked up some magazines and flipped through them. After a while we put them down and picked up some other magazines. It was now 11:25 according to the clock in the room.

42

Quentin said, "I guess Mr. Emple's schedule runs like the railroad's."

I began to think that maybe the old men hadn't been so old when they first started to wait.

"Oh, Mr. Emple." Madam Green-and-Gray spoke to a tall, thin man who had just entered the room. She motioned toward Paul. "This is *Mister* Botts, your 11:10 appointment."

Mr. Emple looked at Paul and said, "There must be some mistake."

I wondered what Paul would say now. Mr. Emple didn't have a friend named Rose.

"There is no mistake," said Paul. That's all he said.

Mr. Emple said, "Come this way, please." He led the way down a long corridor and into his office. His office was like the outer room but his rug was even thicker and his furniture was fancier.

Paul sat down immediately. It is harder to get rid of somebody once he is sitting down. Although that didn't stop Stella Verndale. But I knew from the way Mr. Emple was dressed and the way his office was fixed up that he wouldn't say "scram." Maybe if he were in his sport clothes on a crowded subway and we were both headed for the same empty seat he might. But I bet he never had to take a crowded subway.

Paul introduced Quentin and me. Quentin shook

Mr. Emple's hand and said, "How do you do. Nice place you have here. *Real* nice." Quentin and I sat down, too. Then Mr. Emple sat down. He crossed his legs and sort of folded his hands together.

Every once in a while I am absolutely positive what a person is going to say next. And I was absolutely positive that Mr. Emple was going to say, "What can I do for you?"

Mr. Emple said, "Now, what can I do for you?"

I wish I had been as good at predicting what Quentin would say next. I would have stopped him somehow. He was staring at the rug and the furniture. He said, "Do you make a lot of money here?"

Mr. Emple raised his eyebrows higher than I have ever seen eyebrows raised before. They almost collided with his hair. That is, the gray section of his hair. He had a rim of gray hair that looked like a bush, which surrounded a rim of black hair that looked like a bush, which surrounded some bare skin. It seemed as if a gardener, instead of a barber, had worked on his head. It was the only head of hair I've ever seen that looked landscaped. And on him it looked O.K. Distinguished, my mother would say.

Mr. Emple's eyebrows came down and he said to Quentin, "How old are you, son?"

"That question," said Paul, "is irrelevant, immaterial and should be stricken from the record."

Paul, Quentin and I had been watching reruns of *Perry Mason* on TV, and Paul seemed pleased that the legal information he had picked up had come in so handy so soon in the appointment.

"You're right," said Mr. Emple. "Let's get down to business. Exactly what *is* your business?"

"We have come in behalf of a chicken," said Paul.

"A chicken?" Mr. Emple raised his eyebrows higher than before. I wouldn't have thought it possible. "I don't know what you've heard about our firm," he said, "but most of our clients are large corporations. As a matter of fact, one of our clients is a chicken conglomerate. They market chicken soups, stews, frozen dinners — that sort of thing. A giant company. Now tell me, are you referring to one *single, solitary* chicken?"

"One *single, solitary* chicken who needs a lawyer," said Paul. "You don't want to take the case?"

"It isn't that we don't want to take the case," said Mr. Emple. "It's simply that I don't think *you* would want *us*. Fuller, Fox, Alpert, Hirsch, Hollingsworth & Emple has had no experience whatsoever with a — well, to put it bluntly, with a client who lives in a coop."

Mr. Emple looked at his watch. He moved around in his chair. I could tell that he was wishing we would leave. There was something constantly busy about him. As if he woke up in the morning busy, went to bed busy, and was busy all the time in between.

Paul said, "How do you think Clarence Darrow got where he got? By turning down unusual cases? Why, he would have jumped at the chance to take on a case like this. He would have considered it a real challenge."

Mr. Emple looked at his watch again. Then he looked at the ceiling as if he were trying to remember something. Then he said, "There was a fascinating case — went all the way up to the Supreme Court — *Becker* v. *Pecker*. Seems that a wealthy woman who was fond of chickens left all her money — half a million dollars — to her pet chicken, and her relatives were up in arms about it. They tried to break the will and a couple of them tried to murder the chicken. With an ax, I believe. So a full-time guard was assigned to it. The relatives had a dozen lawyers on the case. Absolutely fantastic case. The chicken won, if I recall correctly."

"A triumph for all the little people of the world," said Paul. "Now about our chicken case. There's a woman in my neighborhood who is trying to persecute a chicken."

"Why would she do that?" asked Mr. Emple. "Is the chicken bothering her?"

"I'll say," said Quentin. "The chicken walks

all over her lawn, eats her plants, drops feathers — "

Sometimes, like every hour on the hour, I wondered why Paul wanted Quentin along with us. But Paul had always liked Quentin and even admired him. Quentin usually came right out and said what he thought without figuring out the angles first. Quentin was a plunger. I think that secretly Paul wanted to be a plunger, too, but he knew he never could be because he wasn't made that way.

Mr. Emple's eyebrows had risen again. "This chicken you want me to represent is engaged in an unlawful act," he said. "She is damaging property that belongs to someone else."

Mr. Emple stood up. This is something grownups do when they want somebody to leave but are too polite to come out and say so. It's a signal that nobody admits is a signal. Paul stuck to his chair as if he were glued to it. Mr. Emple sat down.

"There must be loopholes in the law," said Paul. "This is a very sad case. A nasty woman against a helpless chicken."

"I want you to understand that I *am* sympathetic toward your problem," said Mr. Emple, "but the law is the law."

"If that Supreme Court chicken had you for a lawyer," said Quentin, "she wouldn't have won a cent."

47

"*That* chicken wasn't breaking the law," said Mr. Emple. "*Your* chicken is." He looked at the ceiling again. Then he said, "Your chicken could certainly be defended on the grounds of ignorance of the law but you or your parents would still be held liable because you own her."

"Oh, we don't own her," said Quentin. "She belongs to Mrs. Richardson."

"Mrs. Richardson?" said Mr. Emple. "Who is Mrs. Richardson?"

"Wow!" said Quentin. "That's some question. Well, you see she's got this house on Sycamore Lane and inside it there's — "

Paul interrupted. "Mrs. Richardson is a woman who owns a chicken," he said.

"That's not all she owns," said Quentin.

Now Paul was the one moving around in his chair. I started to squirm, too. I think we both had the same idea that it was a perfect time to leave. Any minute now it might be too late.

Paul stood up. I stood up. Quentin looked surprised. But he stood up, too. Mr. Emple stayed seated.

"We must go," said Paul.

"I would very much like to help you," said Mr. Emple, "but the law is the law."

Paul and I started moving toward the door.

"I like to help youngsters," said Mr. Emple. "I've been a Boy Scout leader for several years."

Paul and I moved closer to the door. "We must go," said Paul.

"I'm also a coach for the Little League," said Mr. Emple.

Paul put one foot out into the corridor. Mr. Emple stayed seated.

And there they were, Paul and Mr. Emple, like two actors who had forgotten their lines. Paul needed an exit cue, but Mr. Emple didn't seem about to give it to him.

Suddenly Quentin walked over to Mr. Emple and shook his hand. Paul and I held our breath. "You're a nice man, after all," said Quentin.

Mr. Emple broke out in a smile that traveled east and west clear across his face. It was every bit as great as his eyebrows' trip north. Then he stood up. "I like to see young people become involved in the world around them," he said. "Fuller, Fox, Alpert, Hirsch, Hollingsworth & Emple encourages that sort of thing. Good day and good luck." He shook hands with Paul and me, and with Quentin for the third time. Then he looked at his watch. Paul, Quentin and I said good-bye and left.

6

We walked down the long corridor. Madam
Green-and-Gray was back on the switchboard with Rose. Paul opened the door and we
walked out. We took the elevator down silently.
When we got to the lobby we started to talk.

"We didn't accomplish anything," I said.

"Yes, we did," said Quentin. "We found out that
Miss America is a lawbreaker."

"Well, I'm not glad we found *that* out," I said.

"Every bit of information we pick up can be
important," said Paul. "Unfortunately, Mr. Emple's information was not particularly cheering. I
was counting on him to stop that petition."

"What do we do now?" I asked.

"We take the 12:20 train home," said Paul. "We
promised."

We walked out of the lobby. Then we were back
on Madison Avenue and in the crowds of people.
It was around lunchtime now and the crowds were

bigger than before. Quentin said, "I wonder what it takes to be noticed in this city. If I rode piggyback on one of you, would that do it? What if I yelled as loud as I could? Or real fast pinched a dozen people in a row? Would anybody pay attention? I bet they wouldn't. They'd just keep on going forever and ever. Maybe they would stop for the Don't Walk sign, but that's all."

Paul wasn't interested in the people or in Quentin's remarks. In fact, he had had an overdose of Quentin's remarks for the day. I could tell that his mind was working furiously. That is, more furiously than usual. We were in a give-up situation and Paul wasn't a give-up type. I am. Once I wanted Roland Rapoport to be my friend and I practically fell on my face for him but he still wouldn't be friends. That was a give-up situation. And I've been in plenty of others. Sometimes you can't win.

We got to Grand Central in time to catch the 12:20 train. The moment I set foot on the train I felt terrible. Terrible that the visit was over, and terrible that there would never be another visit just like it. Never the three of us and Mr. Emple and the chicken business and even Madam Green-and-Gray. It had been terrific and different and I wanted there to be more of it. It was still there — New York — and soon we would be going farther and farther away from it. I wished we had tried to get permission to stay longer. Maybe Paul could talk his mother into talking our mothers into letting us go back soon. And without such a strict time limit.

Paul was still thinking and Quentin was busy admiring his timetables. He had taken a seat by himself in front of Paul and me and had spread all the timetables on the seat beside him. He was talking to himself. "Bridgeport, Port Chester, East Bronx, West Bronx, Hastings, Irvington, Ossining, Brewster, Tarrytown, Yonkers, Scarsdale, Chappaqua, Tuckahoe, New Haven." A line of people was straggling down the aisle, and a fat man stopped beside Quentin and started to sit down. Quentin grabbed most of the timetables but the man sat on Chappaqua and Tuckahoe. "Clumsy," said Quentin. The man unfolded a newspaper and began to read. For him Quentin didn't exist.

The train started up and I leaned back in my seat. I closed my eyes so I could be alone with my trip. After a while I felt dreamy and lazy and under the spell of the train. Paul broke my spell. Suddenly he was back in shape again, raring to go. After his experience with Mr. Emple I thought he might retire. "I'm convinced that we can't stop the petition," he said. "Therefore we will have to take a chance and close in on Mrs. Richardson tomorrow. It will be risky, but we have no choice. This is what we'll do. Quentin, turn around and listen."

I whispered, "The man beside Quentin will hear us."

"The man beside Quentin is in his own world," said Paul. "People who read newspapers on trains are programmed to get off at their correct station, and nothing going on around them penetrates their consciousness from the time they open the newspaper until the time they arrive at their destination."

Quentin turned to the man and said "clumsy" again. It made him feel better, and if the man couldn't hear him, he didn't have anything to lose.

Paul went on. "My plan will commence early tomorrow morning. *Very* early. Around five I would say."

"I'm asleep at five o'clock," said Quentin. "Only the birds are up then."

"The birds and spies," said Paul. "It is a proven fact that espionage flourishes while the world snores."

"I never snore," said Quentin.

Paul looked as if he were about to give a talk on the subject of snoring. But instead he said, "My plan is to watch Mrs. Richardson's house, to follow her when she goes out and to note all her activities, however minor. The three of us will meet outside my house tomorrow morning at 5:20. Are there any questions?"

"Yes," said Quentin. "How in the world can I leave my house at five o'clock in the morning?"

"I am sure you'll be able to think of a way," said Paul. "Resourcefulness is one of the hallmarks of a successful investigator."

"Are we investigators?" I asked. It sounded even better than detectives.

"What else?" said Quentin. "Of course. Investigators. That's us."

The man who was sitting beside Quentin folded his paper, got up and walked out. I will never know if his head was full of the triple-murder story his paper had been opened to or Paul's plans for investigating Mrs. Richardson.

Our stop was next. We got out and walked home from the station. Paul and Quentin left me at my house. My mother had lunch waiting for me. She gave me an even better welcome than Columbus got from Isabella after his first trip. She seemed amazed that I had survived.

"I cooked some lovely liver just for you," she said. The food that doesn't taste good always comes with a description.

"Tell me about everything," she said. And I did,

except for the part where Quentin nearly spilled the beans about Mrs. Richardson.

I spent the afternoon making the trip to New York all over again in my mind. My father was home in time for supper so my mother told him all about the trip. Through the tomato juice, the salad, the meat loaf and the lime sherbet my mother traveled nonstop. It was my fourth New York trip of the day. Once when I really went, once when I told my mother about it, once when I took it in my mind, and now when my mother told my father about it. Anyway, this was a great opportunity for me to keep quiet. Now that I had become an investigator, I was determined to keep my mouth closed as much as possible.

I went to bed early because I knew I was getting up at five o'clock. I also wanted to be by myself to think about the next day. It was lucky that Paul had discovered the spy during summer vacation because it would have been complicated to go to school and be an investigator at the same time. I wondered if I should wear any special clothes. Paul hadn't said anything about that so I decided to wear my regular play clothes.

At last I could feel myself getting tired. I have a kind of alarm clock in my mind, so I set it to go off at five o'clock. Usually I wake up about half an hour earlier than the time I set, but I didn't want to take any chances so I set it for five anyway.

When I woke up the next morning, I grabbed my watch. It was five o'clock. The day had started off just right.

7

I dressed fast and went downstairs to the kitchen. I ate some cereal and then walked slowly to the back door. I couldn't make up my mind whether I wanted to be discovered or not. If I was discovered and I gave a good excuse, maybe I could use the same excuse for the next morning. If I wasn't discovered, I would have to worry all over again the next morning that I would be discovered.

While I was trying to decide, my mother came downstairs. "It's five o'clock in the morning," she said.

"Ten past five," I said.

"All right, ten past five. Where are you going at ten past five?" she asked.

"I can't tell you."

"Well, if you could tell me would I like it?"

"I don't know if you'd exactly *like* it," I said, "but you wouldn't *not* like it."

"You're trying to confuse me."

"True," I said. "The fact of the matter is that I'm an investigator."

"Oh," said my mother. "Why didn't you say so? And where and whom are you investigating at ten past five?"

"Would an investigator tell?" I asked. "Just remember, Mother, that espionage flourishes while the world snores."

"Oh, Paul is an investigator also? Good, good," said my mother.

It's strange how you can never quote Paul and get away with it as your own idea.

"Well," said my mother, "since Paul will be with you, you can go."

I ran all the way to Paul's house. He and Quentin were outside waiting for me.

"How did you guys get away?" I asked.

"I told my mother I was going to be with Paul," said Quentin. "And she said 'Good, good.' "

Paul didn't say how he managed to get out. He probably told his parents he was going to do something physical or menial. He was as excited as the day before, only this time he was excited about a bush.

"Mrs. Richardson has a truly magnificent bush in her side yard," he said. "We can hide behind it and get a good view of the front of her house, an excellent view of the side of her house and a fair view of the back of her house. I gave a trial look this morning."

"This morning?" said Quentin. "What time did you get up?"

"Before the birds," said Paul. "Much before the birds. Now let's get going. We'll go to Mrs. Richardson's house through backyards. She might see us if we approach her bush from the front."

Quietly we crept through a few yards. We had to climb one fence two times — once going into a yard, once going out. I tore my shirt and my sneakers got wet from the grass but an investigator can't expect to stay neat. I don't know why we couldn't have used the street for most of the walk, but I guess that streets are for ordinary people going ordinary places.

And there it was — The Spy House! 51 Sycamore Lane. My heart began to beat faster. I liked that. Like the ripped shirt and wet sneakers, it was part of being an investigator.

The bush that Paul had told us about was on the border between Mrs. Richardson's property and Stella Verndale's. I could see where the grass was different on each side of the bush. So we were at the bush before we actually stepped foot on Mrs. Richardson's land. Paul had that figured out in advance, too. He called it easy access.

The three of us crouched behind the bush as

best we could, but there wasn't much room. In his trial look, Paul should have looked *at* the bush, not away from it. I kept watching to see if somebody's foot or arm was sticking out. It was hard not to have something sticking out because the bush was so small. It was also ugly. It looked like an overgrown head of romaine lettuce going bad.

The worst problem with the hiding place was that there was nothing to do there. How long can you stare at a house that is just sitting on a piece of land?

Quentin kept glancing at his watch. At last he said, "I'm hungry." It was only six o'clock, but suddenly I was hungry, too.

Paul took a package from under his jacket.

"Tuna fish, salami, peanut butter and jelly, roast beef, cream cheese on date-nut bread or bologna?" he asked.

Paul had six sandwiches.

"My mother made them," he said.

"This morning?" asked Quentin.

"Yes," said Paul in a voice that he tried to make sound matter-of-fact. He knew we were impressed. Not only did his mother let him out before the birds were up, but she made him sandwiches to boot. And they were delicious.

"That was great," said Quentin after we had

finished eating. "Your mother is a great sandwich-maker. What do we do next?"

"We continue to watch the house," said Paul. "We are not here for fun and games."

"But nothing is happening," I said. "And my legs are getting cramps. There are only two positions I can put them in, and my body is complaining about both positions."

"Physical discomfort is — " Paul started to talk, but Quentin interrupted.

"Hurts," said Quentin. "Hurts. My body is complaining, too."

"It's unfortunate that Mrs. Richardson doesn't have a larger bush," said Paul. "This one seems to accommodate only one person comfortably." He sighed. "Very well. We shall move forward. About twenty feet, I'd say. We will go up to the house and look in a window. We can crawl, walk or run. Crawling takes the longest time but has the advantage of keeping us low to the ground. Walking will attract the least attention should someone pass by. Running, of course, is the fastest but it is also the noisiest. Now here is another opportunity to have three heads at work. We shall vote."

It took longer for Paul to make his speech than for us to vote and run to a window. We all voted for run because we felt like exercising our legs.

Paul forgot to put that reason in his speech.

We crouched outside the window, and slowly, very slowly, raised our heads and peered inside the house.

"Wow!" whispered Quentin.

I almost said "wow" myself. For there was Mrs. Richardson at her shortwave radio! She was sitting sideways to us and she had headphones on and she was talking. The window was open a crack but we couldn't hear what she was saying.

This was my first look at Mrs. Richardson. She reminded me of a painting I have seen on calendars of a woman with a shawl sitting in a rocking chair, even though Mrs. Richardson wasn't wearing a shawl and she certainly wasn't rocking. It was a peculiar sight. She looked as if she had accidentally wandered in from long, long ago, found the radio and headphones and was radioing for help to get back to her own time.

I was afraid to stare too long at any one time. In fact, Paul, Quentin and I would take a peek, duck, then take another peek. Once in a while Mrs. Richardson turned her head in our direction, and we ducked so fast you could almost hear the air swish. I got enough looks to see that Mrs. Richardson had blue, blue eyes and lots of interesting paths and corners in her face.

This was a very big moment for Paul. We had found Mrs. Richardson actually using her shortwave radio. I think Paul wanted to shout he was so happy, but he was forced to whisper.

"Beautiful, beautiful," he whispered.

"Caught with the goods," whispered Quentin. "What now?"

Quentin was always ready for the next step. Paul glared at him. Paul liked to get every last bit from a situation before going on. And Quentin was spoiling it for him.

As it happened, it didn't make much difference, because Mrs. Richardson took care of the next step. She took off her headphones, turned off her set, put on her hat, got her dog and left the house. It happened almost as fast as I'm telling about it.

Without taking an official vote, we started to follow her.

8

I have seen people following other people on television and in the movies, but it is not the same as following someone on a street like Sycamore Lane. In the movies and on TV there are always doorways to slide into and stores to go in and out of, and all kinds of chances to hide in tricky ways. In the Sycamore Lane neighborhood the houses are set too far back to use the doorways, and the only things you can hide behind are trees, fire hydrants and, on garbage collection day which this wasn't, garbage cans.

We had to stay at least half a block behind Mrs. Richardson, and every time she turned a corner I had a feeling she would vanish forever. But when we got to the corner and turned it, there she was up ahead with her dog pulling her.

Then we got a surprise. We turned a corner and found her walking toward us.

"She's coming back!" I gasped.

"Don't panic," said Paul. "Turn around and walk slowly. Then walk faster. Then run. Let's get back to her house before she does."

We got back to the house a short time before Mrs. Richardson returned. Back to the house, back to the Cramp Bush, and back to nothing to do except look at the house.

Suddenly from across the yard something white came zigzagging toward us, shedding feathers along the way.

"It's Miss America," said Paul. "She's molting."

Quentin took one look at Miss America and fell in love. "Wow!" he said. "She is *cute*! Chicken, here, chicken. Come here, you nice chicken."

"Quiet," said Paul. "We don't want her here. She might give away our hiding place."

But Miss America kept on coming. She headed straight for us, or I should say straight for our bush. Then I found out why the bush looked so sick. It was a snack for Miss America. She pecked away at it in short, quick jerks.

"Go away," I whispered. "Shoo!"

"Scram, you cute thing," said Quentin.

Every time we said something, she moved away cluck-cluck-clucking. And every time she came back.

"Don't say anything," said Paul. "It only gets her excited. When she's excited, she clucks more."

"If she stays here much longer she'll eat away our hiding place," said Quentin.

Miss America pecked away for a few more minutes. Then she strutted over to Quentin and sort of flew onto his lap. "Nice chicken," said Quentin and he patted her. She flapped her wings, hopped off and wandered away. She left three feathers with Quentin and more under the bush. The bush looked a little smaller than before. It made me feel more cramped than ever.

"I vote to crawl, run or walk to the window," said Quentin.

"Not now," said Paul. "We're much safer here. However, if nothing happens soon, we'll be forced to reconsider the window."

Time went by as if it were made of lead. Finally there was some action. The mailman was out in front with a package, and Miss America was waddling down the walk to greet him. "Quick," said Paul, tugging at my arm. "You and I are going up to the mailman and find out where that package is from. I'll talk to him while you peek. Peek fast so Mrs. Richardson won't catch us."

"What about me?" asked Quentin. He started to stretch out. He was hoping to have the bush to himself for a while.

"You will remain hidden," said Paul. "That way we will be certain there is one of us that Mrs. Richardson hasn't seen. You will be more useful in future assignments if you are unseen and unknown."

"I will be the trump card," said Quentin. His mother plays bridge with my mother.

"You mean ace in the hole," said Paul.

"I know what I mean," said Quentin. He was suddenly mad. "I mean I'm going home."

"Look, Quentin," said Paul. "We need you as an investigator. And we need you as a friend. Aren't we friends, Quentin? Aren't we?"

"I'm a friend and I'm a trump card," said Quentin. "What do you know about cards, Paul?"

"I must admit that cards are one of my weak areas of knowledge," said Paul. "Actually I know very little about cards."

I couldn't imagine Paul knowing very little about anything, but I kept quiet. Quentin seemed happy.

Paul and I had to run up to the mailman. Paul had spent so much time talking to Quentin that we had almost missed the mailman altogether. As it was, he was practically at Mrs. Richardson's front door.

"Hello," said Paul. "Tell me, is it true that neither snow nor rain nor heat nor gloom of night can stay you from the swift completion of your appointed rounds?"

"What's that?" said the mailman.

I sneaked a look at the package he was carrying.

It had a postmark and return address but I couldn't make them out. I looked closer. Paul kept on talking.

"I was wondering," he said, "if neither snow nor rain nor heat nor gloom of night can stay you from the swift completion of your appointed rounds. I understand that is propaganda put out by your 33rd Street office."

"Could be," said the mailman. "Sounds real fine, doesn't it?"

I looked closer at the package. I still couldn't make out the postmark but I saw the return address was written in a foreign language. I stood up and kicked Paul.

"Thank you for the information," he said to the mailman. "And keep up the good work. Oh, and remember me to the 33rd Street office."

"Sure," said the mailman. "Any time."

Paul and I hustled off to our hiding place just as Mrs. Richardson opened her door for the mailman.

"I hope she didn't see us," I said. "I found out that the package is definitely from a foreign country. I couldn't tell which one."

"I knew it!" said Paul. "We've got to find out what's inside that package. To the window. Fast!"

Paul, Quentin and I ran to the window. The timing was great. Mrs. Richardson was just opening her package. Inside the package was a box, and inside that box was a smaller box. From inside the smaller box she took out something wrapped in silver foil. It was an orange-yellow color and it was round. She sniffed it and took a small bite out of it.

"Cheese," I whispered. "It looks like cheese."

"Ingenious," whispered Paul. "I'm certain there is something besides cheese in that cheese. She will nibble her way into a hidden message."

Mrs. Richardson took another tiny bite.

I watched her closely. I didn't dare move. I had never before been so interested in watching someone eat a piece of cheese.

Just then a man walked up the front path. He wasn't exactly a man. He was sort of an old boy. He rang the bell. Mrs. Richardson let him in. She took him straight to her shortwave radio. We strained to hear what they were saying, but we couldn't catch a word. They took turns with the headphones. After a while they went into the kitchen. Mrs. Richardson took the cheese with her. We ran around to the kitchen window but the shade was pulled down most of the way. From what we could see, Mrs. Richardson was giving him lunch. She showed him the cheese, and he shook his head no. Maybe messages weren't his favorite kind of food. Mrs. Richardson put the cheese on a counter. We watched them eat, but nothing special happened. I noticed that the boy-man really hogged the poppy seed rolls but that didn't seem too important. Miss America was under the table eating the crumbs as they dropped.

Then out of the blue Quentin whispered, "What time do we quit for the day?"

It was only eleven o'clock, but as I've said, Quentin likes to look ahead.

"Quit?" whispered Paul. "Quit? What do you think this is — a nine-to-five job?"

"Is it a five-to-five job round the clock?" asked Quentin. He forgot to whisper.

"Exactly," said Paul. "We've got to keep at it while we can. Remember the petition." He forgot to whisper, too.

"I have to be home for supper," said Quentin.

"Me, too," I said.

"Complications, complications," said Paul. "Do you think Mrs. Richardson stops her activities at suppertime?"

"We can hope so," said Quentin, "because I definitely have to be home for supper."

"Me, too," I said again.

"Very well," said Paul. "We're in this together. We'll stop at suppertime and we will resume at 5:20 tomorrow morning."

Now I was especially glad my mother knew about my leaving early.

"What about lunch?" asked Quentin. "I'm hungry again."

"Are you going to tell me you have to be home for lunch, too?" asked Paul.

"No, but my mother will want to know where I am," said Quentin. "And where I'm eating."

"Mine, too," I said.

"The solution is simple," said Paul in a way that made it seem as if the problem was hard. "I'll go home and get some sandwiches and bring them back for us. While I'm home I will call your mothers and tell them we're having a picnic on Sycamore Lane and that you will be home for supper. I'll be back soon. Watch the house while I'm gone."

"Wait," said Quentin. "Are you taking orders for lunch? I'd like some lettuce with the bologna. But make sure it's dry or the bologna and bread will get soggy."

I don't know if Paul heard. He was already on his way out of the yard. This whole conversation took place under Mrs. Richardson's kitchen window. I shouldn't have worried about not being able to hear what went on inside her house. I should have been thankful she couldn't hear what was going on *outside*.

Mrs. Richardson's guest left before Paul got back. I wondered if Quentin and I should follow him, but Paul had said to watch the house. Besides, Paul would be back soon with all those sandwiches.

He was gone a long time. At least it seemed

that way. When he finally got back he had sandwiches *and* drinks *and* cookies. His mother was
a real sport. We dug right into the food. We
demolished it.

"I have messages from your mothers," said
Paul. "Both messages are the same. They send
their love and they said not to eat too many
sweets. Did anything happen here while I was
gone?"

We started to tell him that Mrs. Richardson's
guest had left when we noticed that Mrs. Richardson was leaving, too. She was going down the
front walk.

We followed her, using the same method as before. It was a little easier this time because she
went out of the neighborhood and into a shopping
center. She walked past a few stores and then she
walked into the A&P.

We stopped outside the A&P. "Here's your
chance, Quentin," said Paul. "She doesn't know
you. Follow her!"

And I said, "Do your stuff, Quentin."

Quentin didn't say one word. He just walked
quickly into the A&P.

Paul and I watched from the outside. The windows were wide, and by moving around we had
a pretty clear view of the aisles except toward the
back of the store.

We saw Quentin take up his position, falling in

step behind Mrs. Richardson. He kept quite a bit behind her. Then he kept even farther behind. He raised his head. He looked as if he were sniffing. Sometimes both he and Mrs. Richardson moved out of sight. At other times we could see one or the other. And a couple of times we saw Mrs. Richardson coming down one aisle and Quentin going up another aisle where she had just been. Then it was like watching a cardboard game with two pieces moving along trails, one piece gliding ahead toward the goal and the other trailing behind, losing.

Mrs. Richardson stopped at the fish counter. Quentin was hanging out in baked beans and soups and he looked as if he didn't know what to do next. He stood there for a short time and then started to walk. He saw Mrs. Richardson just as she headed for the check-out counter. He got bold and went right behind her. Mrs. Richardson unloaded her wagon at the counter. Quentin watched while he pretended not to watch. He picked up a magazine with an absolutely spectacular-looking woman on the cover. Quentin was not interested in magazines that had spectacular-looking women on their covers.

Then his eyes opened very wide. But it wasn't because of the cover. He was staring at the check-out clerk. And no wonder. He was the same boy-man who had had lunch at Mrs. Richardson's house! Paul and I should have recognized him earlier, but we had been too busy watching Mrs. Richardson and Quentin.

Mrs. Richardson was talking to the checker, and Quentin was leaning over, listening. Quentin opened his mouth. Paul got all tense beside me. He was sending a brain-wave message to Quentin. "Don't say it. Please don't say it. Not 'wow.' Not now."

Quentin must have gotten the message. He kept his mouth open, but nothing came out of it.

Mrs. Richardson paid the checker, he put her groceries in a bag and she walked out. Paul and I ran into a beauty parlor next door to hide. Mrs. Richardson passed by. Then Quentin walked by, looking every which way for us while still trailing Mrs. Richardson. We left the beauty parlor just as a lady with hair like a bright orange mountain was about to chase us out. We caught up with Quentin. We talked while we walked.

"Did you see the checker?" he asked. "He's the guy she had for lunch! And she spoke to him in a foreign language!" Quentin was almost shouting. "A foreign language! She was passing secrets."

"How do you know she was passing secrets?" I asked.

"It figures," said Quentin. "It just figures."

"Do you know what language it was?" asked Paul.

74

"No," said Quentin. He sounded tired all of a sudden.

"Frustrating. Frustrating," said Paul. "I should have taken a chance and gone in myself. But you did very well, Quentin. An excellent piece of work. Excellent."

"Thanks," said Quentin. "I used strategy, you know. I figured out how to keep track of her. I could smell her perfume aisles away."

"I know," said Paul. "It's called Dangerous Drift. My mother uses it. Imported from France and fantastically overpriced."

"There was only one time I couldn't find her," said Quentin. "When she was at the fish counter. I couldn't smell the Dangerous Drift over the fish."

"What are her buying habits?" asked Paul.

"You mean what did she buy?" asked Quentin. "She didn't buy anything special. But she drinks gallons of coffee, I think. She bought instant, regular, freeze-dried and low caffeine. I don't think that's healthy, do you? She also bought fish, of course, and dog food, spaghetti, detergent and prune yogurt."

Just as Quentin was saying "prune yogurt," I noticed that Mrs. Richardson wasn't in front of us anymore. She wasn't anywhere. "She must have gone inside one of the stores," said Quentin.

We peeked through windows. Now I was getting very professional at that. We found Mrs. Richardson in a bank.

"The bank!" said Paul. "She told me she doesn't trust banks."

"And we don't trust Mrs. Richardson, right?" said Quentin.

"Right," said Paul. "And we are *all* going into the bank. Quentin, she might remember you from the supermarket, but even if she does, it is not unusual for you to show up at a bank that is just a few doors away. So you will stand right behind her in line again. Watch her very closely."

"Where will the two of you be?" asked Quentin.

"We will bend low over the writing counter," said Paul. "That way we hope we can hear but not be seen. Let's go."

We walked inside and took our places. Quentin got close behind Mrs. Richardson. There was one person ahead of her. Then it was Mrs. Richardson's turn. She spoke to the teller. "I have been informed by a reliable source," she said, "that your bank pays interest at an annual rate of 5½ percent, posted quarterly and computed from the day of deposit. Your literature verifies this information. Therefore, I would like to open an account and deposit $20,000."

Quentin opened his mouth and said "Wow!"

It was a terrible moment. Paul and I closed our eyes. But that didn't help. So we opened them.

Mrs. Richardson whirled around and leaned toward Quentin like a steamroller about to flatten a bump. Then she said, "Are you following me, young man?"

Quentin couldn't think of a word to say. He couldn't even think of no because no would be a lie. And Quentin's first thoughts were never lies. At last he said, "Well, I'm standing behind you."

Mrs. Richardson said, "And you were standing behind me at the check-out counter at the supermarket. And you were walking behind me before that. And for all your walking, up one aisle and down another, what did you finally check out? A bag of peanuts. Now you're behind me at the bank. Would you mind telling me what you're doing at the bank?"

Poor Quentin. The only times he had been in a bank were with his mother. And usually all he did there was collect blank deposit and withdrawal slips, which looked official enough to replace the lost money in his Monopoly game. He didn't know anything about bank business.

Then he remembered Paul's bank account. "I came to check on a friend's bank account," he said. "And if you don't believe it, you can follow *me*."

Quentin walked up to a teller who had no people in line. He spoke up in a loud voice. "I'm a friend — a *good* friend — of Paul H Botts, who has an account in this bank, and I would like to know how much money he has in it."

"I'm sorry," the teller said, "but we can't give that information to you. Have your friend come in himself."

"He's already — " Quentin said and then he caught himself. "I will certainly do that," he said. "And thank you very much anyway."

Then he turned to Mrs. Richardson. "A *real* friend and a *real* account," he said. And he walked out of the bank fast.

Mrs. Richardson turned to her teller. While her back was to us, Paul and I left.

The three of us met outside. "Let's get out of here fast," said Quentin.

"This way," said Paul. And we ran into a Laundromat. There was a loud song coming from a speaker, and the jangling and the jumping sounds were like theme music for our situation.

"I blew my cover," said Quentin.

"It doesn't matter," said Paul. "We don't have to watch her anymore. We've seen all we have to see. We know all we have to know. Mrs. Richardson is a spy. Up to ten minutes ago there was still one missing part, but it is no longer missing."

Paul waited for us to ask what the missing part had been. Quentin and I looked at each other hoping for hints. But it was Paul's missing part, and here with the music blasting and the laundry twirling around in the machines he was going to announce it.

"The missing part was the motive," he said finally. "I will explain."

There was another wait while Paul shifted his feet and cleared his throat. Paul believed that the longer you had to wait for something, the better it seemed after you got it. I didn't feel that way. I felt like the ladies waiting for their laundry to come out of the washers and dryers. Whether it came out sooner or later, it was still the same stuff.

At last Paul got going again. He said, "Mrs. Richardson is wearing a wedding ring. Since there is no man around, I presume she is widowed. And at present she has no visible means of support."

"No job, huh?" said Quentin.

"No job," said Paul. "And she told me that most of her money is invested in the stock market. Stock market values on the whole have deteriorated drastically in the past few months. I would conclude that Mrs. Richardson lost money. However, at the same time, she has taken on considerable expenses. For example, mortgage payments on her house, taxes, general upkeep — "

"Dangerous Drift perfume," said Quentin.

"That, too," said Paul. "Mrs. Richardson needs money. Or to be more accurate, Mrs. Richardson *needed* money. We saw that she just made a deposit of $20,000. That money had to come from somewhere. That money could have come from a foreign country! And I'm certain that it did."

Paul's voice rose above the music and the laundry machines. He stood, not moving, as if someone were taking his picture. Then he said, "We've established her motive. It's a shame that it's money. I could have forgiven misguided patriotism."

As I think back on it, I'm not quite sure just how Mrs. Richardson's motive got established, but since Paul said it did, Quentin and I figured it must be so.

9

We are through for today," said Paul.

"But it's not suppertime," said Quentin.

"True," said Paul. "However, we accomplished so much today that there is only one further thing to do. And the best time to do it is early tomorrow. It will be the most dangerous step of all."

"What will we be doing?" I asked.

"Tomorrow you'll find out," said Paul.

"I vote to find out right now," said Quentin.

"I don't," I said. "You mean we just go home right now and no more Cramp Bush?" I liked that idea.

"That's right," said Paul. "And don't forget. Tomorrow morning at 5:20 outside my house."

We left the Laundromat. It was peaceful outside. We didn't have to follow anybody, and in a way that was peaceful, too. We walked home slowly. We stopped at a luncheonette for sodas. Quentin was thirsty from eating too many pea-

81

nuts, and Paul's throat was dry from his Laundromat speech.

When I finally got to my house, my mother was setting the table for supper. "Hands clean?" she asked. I didn't say anything but I nodded. Now I had plenty to hide, and keeping quiet at suppertime was more important than ever.

"How was your day?" she asked me when she and my father and I had sat down at the table.

"Fine," I said.

"Fine, huh?" she said.

"Yep, fine," I said.

I was getting a little worried. First I had said no words, then I had said one word, then I said two words. I could feel myself getting sucked in. But my mother didn't ask me anything else and she never mentioned the word investigator.

I knew she was curious and if there were such things as padlocks for tongues she probably would have been wearing one to protect herself from herself. She turned to my father and started to talk to him. She kept him busy in conversation. I think it was on purpose so he wouldn't ask me any questions. My mother was O.K. She would have made a good Mata Hari except that Mata Hari didn't look a thing like my mother from what I've heard.

So what happened next was my own fault. My father told my mother that the string beans were stringy. And I told my mother that there were some real good-looking string beans at the A&P. And my father said, "You were in the A&P today?" And I said, "Not exactly *in*. It was more like *at*."

"In. At. What's the difference? Did you break a window at the A&P?"

"No," I said, trying to get back to one-word answers, which I shouldn't have left in the first place.

My father was getting very suspicious. I think he was planning to go around town hunting for broken windows. Maybe if I *had* broken a window I would have been better off. I knew I couldn't last another supper without my father making me tell everything. And probably the only reason I escaped that night was because I ate fast and skipped dessert.

As I left the dining room I heard my father say, "I don't understand it. He loves caramel crunch."

I went to my room but I kept listening for footsteps. I was afraid that my father would come to my room and make me confess. Even though it would be a different confession than he expected.

My father is really a good guy. We spend loads of time together and he takes me places and I can tell that he really wants to. There is something known as Spending Time With One's Children. My mother's bridge club is strong on that idea and they discuss it a lot. Like on Wednesdays they do such and such with their children and on Thursdays they do more such and such, and on Fridays more, and they go on and on. It seems as if the only time they spend away from their children is at the bridge club, from the way they tell it. But my father and I just get together naturally and I don't think he ever heard of it as an idea. So actually I have only one problem with my father. He has very strict opinions about right and wrong that sometimes get in my way. And that was the trouble now. I was sure he wouldn't approve of his son investigating somebody.

Anyway, he didn't come. He was probably still trying to figure out who he owed broken-window money to.

My mother came up late with a dish of caramel crunch. She didn't say anything except "here" and I didn't say anything except "thank you." But we exchanged tremendous smiles.

When I went to bed I couldn't sleep. I was getting used to being an investigator, so that wasn't the reason. It was something else. I was feeling sad about Mrs. Richardson even though she was a spy. Before today she had just been a name that Paul had talked about. Now she was a person with paths and corners in her face and blue, blue eyes. She was probably sleeping now in her wearing-out or worn-out bed, and she didn't know that three people were nosying into her life. And that Stella Verndale was out to get her, too. Maybe I was as bad as Stella.

I was so busy thinking about Mrs. Richardson that I almost forgot to set my mental alarm clock. Just as I was drifting off to sleep, I remembered.

10

I had a dream that I was in school and Mrs. Richardson was my teacher. There was a bunch of us kids she was keeping after school because we were "naughty children." There was Ivan the Terrible, Genghis Khan, Nero, Stella Verndale and me. Mrs. Richardson was making Nero clean the blackboards. Ivan and Genghis were kicking each other and Stella was telling on them. Then Miss America walked in. She was the principal of the school. She walked over to Stella, laid an egg on her head and left. I don't know how she managed to do that since Stella was standing up, but that's the way it is in dreams.

I was sorry when I woke up. It was the most interesting dream I'd had in weeks.

It was another five o'clock on the dot awakening. Everything went smoothly. My mother didn't show up in the kitchen, and I was outside Paul's house by 5:19. He and Quentin were there.

Paul got down to business right away. "Today

we will obtain the evidence," he said. "We will get Mrs. Richardson's notebooks, her foreign mail and her shortwave radio."

"Wow!" said Quentin. "Are we going to take that cheese she got in the mail?"

"I thought of taking it," said Paul, "but I rejected the idea. It is not within easy reach. We will take only the evidence in the shortwave radio room. Besides, we should leave *something* for the FBI to find when they raid her house."

"They're raiding her house?" asked Quentin.

"Certainly," said Paul. "After they get the evidence from us. We will also advise them to put the checker at the A&P under surveillance. I imagine that there is a widespread ring of spies and he is a go-between. He is in a position to be in contact with all kinds of people."

I was afraid to ask the next question, but I couldn't stand not asking. "How are we going to get into her house?"

"Through the window," said Paul, "while Mrs. Richardson is out walking her dog. Now to be perfectly fair, I feel I must advise you that breaking and entering *is* punishable under the law."

I had a real sinking feeling. When I heard the words window and breaking so close together I remembered my father's suspicion. Now I knew it wasn't suspicion. It was a prophecy.

But, as usual, Paul fixed things up with his

words. "I have observed," he said, "that the window is already opened a bit. So we are not *exactly* breaking in."

"But we are exactly breaking the law by entering," I said.

"I am prepared to make that sacrifice for my country," he said. "However, if you two aren't, I'll understand."

"Well, since you put it that way, I'll do it," I said. I knew he put it that way on purpose. So did Quentin. But he said O.K., too.

If I had known beforehand about Paul's plan, I would have set my mental alarm clock for noon and slept right through the whole thing.

We crept through backyards just like the day before. Only this time I didn't like my heart beating so fast. I didn't like anything about being an investigator anymore. I wasn't only scared. I was unhappy. I had been happy all summer, but I hadn't known it until I got to be unhappy just then. Maybe you have to feel the opposite of something before you can really feel the something.

Quentin talked a lot. I think he was scared, too. "Did you bring any sandwiches today?" he asked Paul.

"No, we'll eat when we're finished," said Paul. "This isn't a job for a full stomach."

Suddenly Quentin stopped and asked, "How will we explain to the FBI how we got the stuff?"

It was a good question. It was a terrific question. Now maybe Paul would call everything off.

"The FBI is kind to informers," said Paul. "Especially underage informers. However, I don't think it will be necessary to tell them everything. And, although the idea is repugnant to me, as a last resort there is always the Fifth Amendment."

"I've heard of that," said Quentin. "That's a famous amendment. Wow!"

I knew then that we were going through with it.

We got to Mrs. Richardson's house and went straight to the window. We didn't have long to wait for action. Mrs. Richardson left with her dog almost immediately.

"Our timing was perfect this morning," whispered Paul.

He started to push up the window. It wouldn't give. The three of us put our hands on it. "Steady," said Paul. "Now push!"

We pushed up. Nothing happened. We pushed again. At last the window slid up an inch or so. We pushed again and it went all the way up. We stuck our heads inside. Tiny slivers of wood from the window frame sprinkled into our hair. Paul said, "After we get the notebooks and the mail and the radio, we must run home and wash our hair thoroughly."

I had to give Paul credit. Right in the middle

of a dangerous mission he was already instructing us on getting rid of damaging evidence.

We squeezed through the open window and stepped down into the room. My heart was beating so fast I would have lost count if I'd been keeping track. Why had I tried so hard to get into the house when what I wanted was to be outside and far away?

Compared to mine, Paul's heart was probably in slow motion, but he worked fast. He grabbed most of the notebooks and the mail and the radio. There was practically no work for Quentin and me. At least that's the way it seemed until I saw that the radio Paul grabbed was still sitting on the table. He was sort of leaning over hugging it. "Help!" he said, which is a word he hardly ever uses. "This radio is too heavy for me to lift."

Quentin and I grabbed the radio, too. Paul said, "When I say three, we'll all lift together. One . . . two . . ."

"*Three!*" said a voice that didn't belong to any of us. It was an angry voice and it belonged to Mrs. Richardson.

And that brings me up to and includes the moment when I officially knew I was in a mess.

11

Mrs. Richardson and her dog were in the door-
way of the room. At that instant I didn't
know if I was more afraid of her or her dog, but
I was pretty sure that in the long run it would be
her.

"I imagine that you want a full explanation,"
said Paul.

It was only right that Paul speak first because
this whole business was his idea and Quentin and
I couldn't think of anything to say anyway. I guess
that even "wow" wasn't enough for this occasion.

"I would like you to tell me why you three boys
are in my house at this unholy hour trying to make
off with my notebooks, my mail and my radio,"
said Mrs. Richardson.

I must admit that never in my whole life had I
heard such a reasonable request.

Quentin nudged Paul. "That amendment," he
said. "The famous one. Can we use it?"

"Quiet," said Paul. Then he said to Mrs. Richardson, "It is really a very long, very dull story not worthy of your attention."

"Oh, I think it's worthy of my attention," said Mrs. Richardson. "As a matter of fact, I have been paying quite a bit of attention to portions of your story — the portions that I know about."

"That you know about?" I asked.

"Yes, indeed," said Mrs. Richardson. "I know a very great deal. That is how I was able to trap you."

"This is a trap?" said Paul. "A trap?"

"I'm surprised that a boy of your intelligence doesn't recognize a trap when he's fallen into it," said Mrs. Richardson. "Since you are reluctant to tell the story, I will. It all started early — very early — yesterday morning when I saw three faces pressed against my window. I recognized one face. The one with the wiggleable ears. You didn't think I saw you, did you? Well, I didn't let on. I wanted to see what you would do next. And why. Also, I found the situation quite humorous — *then*."

Mrs. Richardson took a deep breath. Her voice was like a car with engine trouble. It started up O.K. and was smooth for a while. Then it sputtered and stopped. Now it was starting up again.

"I saw you follow me when I walked Melvin," she said. "Your tracking technique was extremely

amateurish. Next I saw two of you with my post-
man. One of you was engaging him in conversation
while the other scrutinized the outside of a package addressed to me. Didn't think I saw that
either? I saw you at the window again when I was
opening my package from the International
Cheese-of-the-Month Club."

"Oh, boy," I whispered to myself. "Regular
cheese." Paul should have known. His mother belonged to that cheese club. Mrs. Richardson's
package couldn't have been more innocent if it had
been a box of mint cookies from the Girl Scouts.

"Then you watched my luncheon guest from the
time he arrived until the time he left," said Mrs.
Richardson. "He knew it, too. Once he almost
choked on his poppy seed rolls. Then you saw us
together later at the A&P. And now you want to
know all about him and my conversation with him
at the check-out counter, don't you?"

The three of us nodded. Mrs. Richardson was
sounding like a very interesting lady from the trap
part on.

"The checker at the A&P is my nephew," said
Mrs. Richardson. "He is studying to be a diplo-
mat. I come from a diplomatic family, although
that is beside the point. My nephew attends the
Berlitz School of Languages, where he is a top
student. He works at the A&P two days a week

and comes to my house for lunch. Since I am a linguist, I help him by checking out my grocery items in the foreign language he is studying at the time. At the moment he is studying Urdu."

"How do you say instant coffee in Urdu?" asked Quentin. He really wanted to know.

"Again beside the point," said Mrs. Richardson in a snappy way that meant that the coffee conversation had begun and ended at the very same time.

"And as for your little A&P adventure," she said, "one of you inside the store, two of you outside. What kind of absurd strategy was that?"

"One if by land, two if by sea," said Quentin, who was feeling patriotic.

Mrs. Richardson continued, "Finally," she said, "I saw all of you inside the bank. By then I was almost chuckling out loud. I did enjoy most of yesterday. But don't get your hopes up that I approve of *anything* you've done. I just couldn't resist speaking out when I heard what's-your-name say 'wow.' What *is* your name, by the way?"

"Quentin," said Quentin.

"Well, when I heard Quentin, I abruptly changed my tactics," said Mrs. Richardson. "I went from the defensive to the offensive, a maneuver which when done correctly can catch one's opponent completely off guard. Right, Quentin?"

"Well, umm," said Quentin. He lowered his head.

"Never mind," said Mrs. Richardson. "The truth is that Quentin here was too clever for me."

Quentin's chin had been moving farther and farther downward. All of a sudden he poked it high into the air.

"He completely outfoxed me," said Mrs. Richardson. "He gave me an explanation so ridiculous that I couldn't answer him. To be that ridiculous, one has to be very, very clever.

"I suppose you want to know why I went to the bank," continued Mrs. Richardson. "It is true that I don't trust banks. But occasionally one has to put one's faith in something more substantial than a cookie jar. Cookie jars, however sturdy and dependable, somehow do not inspire confidence as a repository for $20,000. I received a check for $20,000 in the mail yesterday. You were so involved with my package, you didn't bother with an insignificant little white envelope. I got that money as payment on the sale of my former house. The house was too big for me after my husband died. It was worth a great deal more than I received. But that, too, is beside the point."

I was mixed up. Mrs. Richardson was toppling Paul's clues much faster than he had built them up. I hardly had time to let one piece of information sink in before her voice was off and running with more news. Her engine trouble seemed to be over.

She said, "To conclude the events of yesterday, after I left the bank I saw the three of you in the Laundromat. Paul was making a speech over a basket of laundry as if he were Mark Antony presiding over Caesar's funeral."

Actually Paul had reminded me more of Lincoln delivering the Gettysburg Address but I didn't want to interrupt Mrs. Richardson.

"I walked home," said Mrs. Richardson, "and you didn't follow me. I thought that you had probably had your fill of me and that today you would think of some other foolish thing to do elsewhere. But there you were at my window this morning. I could have caught the three of you then and there, but just as the day before, I decided to wait. I was extremely curious to see if you would follow me again when I left the house with Melvin. But you didn't. That's when I decided to trap you. I took Melvin for the shortest walk possible. To the nearest fire hydrant. Then I came back, thinking at best I would trap you looking in my window, and at worst . . . Do you know that breaking and entering is a crime punishable under the law?"

"It wasn't breaking," said Paul. "The window was open."

"I am prepared to make a sacrifice for my country," said Quentin. "To get the goods on a spy."

"A spy? Is that what you thought I was?" Mrs. Richardson gasped.

"That's what," said Quentin.

Actually, I still wasn't sure that she wasn't a spy. She hadn't explained about her notebooks or why she had a shortwave radio. We hadn't asked her why, but I wasn't about to. It would have been like asking a crocodile to open his mouth wider so I could count his teeth.

But Quentin said, "All kinds of foreign mail, all kinds of notebooks and a shortwave radio."

"A spy?" Mrs. Richardson gasped again. She said the word in a disgusted way, as if she didn't want to have anything to do with it.

There was a long silence. Paul, Quentin and I looked at one another. Now that we had gone this far we had to know the rest.

"I am a linguist," Mrs. Richardson said finally. "I speak ten foreign languages. Five of them extremely well, three of them adequately, and two of them horribly. I am also a traveler. I purchased my shortwave radio in order to improve my proficiency in foreign languages and to make friends around the world and of course to keep in touch with the friends I have. I am a *licensed* shortwave radio operator. However, that really doesn't matter. Since I've moved to Sycamore Lane the static has been ghastly and the only people I've managed

97

to speak to are a Japanese fisherman complaining about his catch and a Turkish belly dancer who promised to send me her recipe for fig soufflé."

Mrs. Richardson went on. "I also have an extensive correspondence with people all over the world. As you have observed. As for my notebooks, I am a person of many interests. Some of my notebooks contain poetry I've written. Unpublished, but I prefer it that way. Some of them hold my collection of recipes. One contains statistics of former dog-walkers that I'm too sentimental to throw away.

"So much for me," said Mrs. Richardson. "And now for you. I think you boys are bored. And I further think that this is one of the reasons you decided I was a spy. It was too boring to think I was just an ordinary woman. Of course I'll grant you that I'm *not* an ordinary woman. But I'm not a spy, either. You can relax, all of you. You will be happy to know that I have decided to forgive you."

"Good," said Quentin. And he started to leave through the open window.

"Wait," said Mrs. Richardson.

I felt myself going stiff.

"Before you go," she said, "I want to tell you something. I *do* know some spies."

"Who?" asked Quentin. "Who?"

"The three of you," said Mrs. Richardson.

"Us? We're investigators," said Quentin. "That's different."

"Nonsense," said Mrs. Richardson. "That's just a highfalutin' label you gave yourselves. It's just a weak excuse for being a snooper. You spied on me. That makes you a spy."

I must admit that what Mrs. Richardson was saying wasn't exactly news to me. I almost had it figured out the night before when I couldn't get to sleep.

"Do you know what privacy is?" asked Mrs. Richardson.

"Of course," said Paul. "My dictionary defines privacy as the state of being private."

"You might get an A on that in school," said Mrs. Richardson, "but you just flunked here. I don't want statements. I want feelings. There is a part of oneself that belongs only to oneself. And no one should try to take that part away from another person. That part is private. I bought this house so that I could have privacy. How would you feel if someone snooped on you, on what you own, on where you go, on what you do and don't do? You tried to take my privacy away. There is a wonderful old saying that goes — "

"I know! I know!" yelled Quentin. "It's mind your own business!"

99

"That wasn't the exact saying I had in mind," said Mrs. Richardson. "But it's better than mine. In fact it's utterly perfect. That part of my business and my life that I want to share with you I will share. The rest is . . ."

She paused, and we three boys said all together, *"private!"*

Well, after Mrs. Richardson made her speech she wasn't mad anymore. In fact she let us listen while she used her shortwave radio. I couldn't understand what was going on because she was talking to the static in several languages. Then she invited us for cocoa, except for Paul who had milk. She told him he could still have the dog-walking job if he wanted it, and he did.

Miss America wandered in and Mrs. Richardson gave Quentin some spaghetti to feed her. Quentin held the spaghetti over Miss America while she jumped for it and got it. It was the kind of trick that only dogs and cats get credit for doing, but Miss America could do it, too. After she ate the spaghetti, she went after Quentin's shoelaces and managed to untie them. She was the first chicken I had ever known and she was great. Even though I hadn't known her long, I knew I was going to miss her if she were taken away.

Mrs. Richardson let her out the door. She made straight for Stella Verndale's lawn and started pecking away.

"There she goes," said Quentin, "breaking the law with every bite."

Paul and I looked at Quentin. Then we all raised our eyebrows. I don't know if we intended to or it just worked out that way.

Suddenly the old familiar look came back to Paul's face. The idea look. I didn't know what he had in mind but it had to be an improvement over his last idea.

"Mrs. Richardson," he said, "your chicken is engaged in an unlawful act. In fact, she is taking away somebody's privacy."

"What?" said Mrs. Richardson.

"Miss America is invading private property," said Paul. "Stella Verndale's lawn, to put it frankly, is none of Miss America's business."

"Hey, what are you saying?" asked Quentin. "You don't like Stella, remember?"

"I don't like Stella, but that doesn't mean she's wrong about *everything*," said Paul.

"You're a regular Benedict Arnold," said Quentin. "How can you say such things?"

"Because they're true," said Mrs. Richardson. "Paul is absolutely right. I had never thought about it that particular way. Perhaps I didn't *want* to think about it that particular way. Paul, you have the mind of a lawyer."

"A lawyer like Mr. Emple," said Quentin.

"Who is Mr. Emple?" asked Mrs. Richardson.

"Funny, he wanted to know who you are," said Quentin.

"Let's discuss Miss America," said Paul.

"Let's," said Quentin. "We can't tell you about Mr. Emple without telling you about the petition."

"You mean that *you* know about the petition?" asked Mrs. Richardson.

"You mean *you* do?" asked Quentin.

"I heard about it from at least three different sources," said Mrs. Richardson. "But it doesn't bother me. I'm too old to be frightened by a piece of paper and that shrieking Stella. Now I presume that this Mr. Emple knows about the petition, too."

"Oh sure," said Quentin. "He's a lawyer and a Boy Scout leader and a Little League coach. You should see his office. Wow! Anyway, we went to his office and — "

"Never mind," said Mrs. Richardson. "I couldn't stand another of your adventures today. Tell me about it some other time when I'm in the mood to listen. Right now I've got to think about Miss America."

"Why don't you build a fence around your yard?" said Paul. "Then Miss America can run free there and eat any of the plants she likes. And a fence will make Stella Verndale seem that much farther away."

"And it could keep out spies, too," said Quentin.

"I'll think about it," said Mrs. Richardson. "In private."

We said good-bye to Mrs. Richardson. It felt much better leaving her house than it had going in. We used the front door.

12

All this happened during the week of July 12. But the week wasn't up yet. I don't know how she got such fast action, but two days later Mrs. Richardson had a fence up. Paul, Quentin and I went over to see it. Miss America seemed satisfied to stay in the yard. She pecked at the fence now and then. Maybe she would get to like it as much as Stella Verndale's plants. Melvin went out and kept her company. Mrs. Richardson looked at them through a window like a proud mother or grandmother or governess or whatever she was to them.

I got my mother to call Stella to ask about the petition. I couldn't wait until the next meeting of the club. Stella told my mother that she had torn up the petition after the fence came. Then she started to complain about how ugly she thought the fence was, but she said that she didn't intend to do anything about it because if the fence came down, the chicken might come back.

Anyway, we had probably worried too much about that petition. Actually, about the only people I know of who would sign a petition for Stella are Ivan the Terrible, Genghis Khan and Nero.

So that's how my composition about the week of July 12 would read if I wrote it. But I'm not going to. Why should I clutter up Miss Nathan's life by telling her things she'd be better off not knowing? Anyway, summer vacation is finished now and that's that, except for a few nice leftovers. Paul spends a lot of time at Mrs. Richardson's house. They exchange a few words in Urdu and listen to the static on her radio. Her radio weighs 133 pounds, by the way. Quentin and I go over there once in a while to play with Miss America. She's really beautiful now. She grew wattles, which are red things on each side of her throat. That means she'll probably be ready to lay her first egg soon. Mrs. Richardson promised Paul, Quentin and me some of the eggs, but she said that Stella Verndale is going to get the very first one.

I wonder if she'd let us deliver it.

About the Author

MARJORIE WEINMAN SHARMAT has published over ninety books for children and young adults, among them *A Visit with Rosalind, The Lancelot Closes at Five, Rich Mitch, Nate the Great,* and *Getting Something on Maggie Marmelstein.*

Most of her stories are inspired by real-life incidents. As a child, Ms. Sharmat and her best friend used to spy on the adults in their neighborhood. Her family even had a pet chicken named Miss America, just like Mrs. Richardson in this story.

Ms. Sharmat used to live at 51 Sycamore Lane, the site of much of this story, but now makes her home with her husband, Mitchell, in Tucson, Arizona. They have two grown sons.